Copyright © 2025 Maddie Evans

AF093372

Chapter One

Emily

I wake up to the TV in my room still on. It's way brighter than it was last night, but that's because my eyes aren't adjusted quite yet.

My husband, Nathan, always forgets to set the sleep timer before going to sleep. He always goes to bed after me since he stays up playing his video games. I could never get into them, they make my brain hurt.

I met my husband at the same school that I work at. He was and still is a very nerdy, yet handsome man. Well, handsome to me.

I'm an elementary school music teacher. It's so much fun seeing all of my students' little faces all day, even though some of the kids I teach are way too hyper for my taste. All of my front row students are usually the most quiet, which makes no sense to me why they would sit in the front of the class, but then again, you barely get caught talking in class if you sit in the back.

I roll over in bed and unplug my phone. *Software Update Required,* my screen reads. I hate updates, they take forever. I push the *Update Later Tonight* option that's on my screen. I always let it update at night, that way I don't have to worry about an emergency call from Nathan while he's at work. I don't have any family that cares about me, so I only have to worry about my husband.

My family and I had a falling out right after I got married. They didn't want me to marry him because they said "You can do better." My parents are rich, so they expected me to marry into wealth and be with, what they consider, an attractive man. They never thought Nathan was good looking enough for me, but I never went for looks. My husband is handsome to me and that's all that matters.

After I'm done checking my usually empty email inbox, I roll over to my husband and kiss him on the cheek, waking him up. I'm always awake before him because I need time to wake up before jumping out of bed. He shifts around and finally opens his eyes, "Good morning" I say, with a high pitched tone in my voice. I know he finds it annoying, but what kind of wife would I be if I didn't annoy my husband? "Morning," he says. He's always a grouch in the mornings until he gets ready for the day and then he's a ball of energy.

I roll back over and grab my phone again, checking on the updates from my show. There is a new episode tonight and I am so excited. I love true crime everything. A show that I've been watching tells true stories of serial killers and unsolved crimes. Sometimes they do interviews with killers if they're not already dead. Nathan thinks that I'm obsessed with killers, but that's not the case. I'm obsessed with their thinking process.

I check the time and realize that if I don't get up now, I'll be late for work. I was up late packing my husband's suitcase. He's going on a small business trip for work this weekend. He always forgets something, so I pack for him every time.

As I'm getting dressed, I noticed that I may have gained a few pounds. I was never the girl with the hot figure all the guys wanted. I've always been petite and sometimes I think that my body never established itself just to screw me over. I don't have big boobs or a nice butt, I'm just flat with some notice that I'm a female.

I brush out my straight, blonde hair and put it up in a ponytail, my usual hairstyle. I never learned how to do my hair or makeup, so I just go with the basics.

I can hear Nathan shuffling around in the bathroom that's attached to our room. "Are you almost ready to go?" I yell through the door. Even though we work separate jobs, we like to leave our apartment together. We aren't breakfast people, so that saves a ton of time in the mornings. He finally opens the door. "Let's go," he says, walking past me, grabbing his suitcase. He's not his usual energetic self this morning, I wonder if he didn't sleep well. Something is off with him, but he ignores me when I ask him about it.

Chapter Two

Nathan

I usually don't mind when my wife wakes me up with that high pitched voice, but today just made me upset. I know it shouldn't make me upset because she just wants me to smile.

I get out of bed and head to the bathroom to get ready for the day. It's a big day for me. I have a few meetings and then right after those, I'm going on a business trip. It was kind of a last minute thing, but I decided to go through with it anyway.

One good thing I can say about Emily is that she doesn't take two hours to get ready like other women do. She doesn't do her makeup and her hair is always up in a ponytail. She cares about me on a level that I don't think I could feel with someone else.

"Are you almost ready to go?" I hear Emily yell at me through the door. After a few seconds, I open the bathroom door. "Let's go" I say. I'm just annoyed today. I feel my head buzzing and I can't seem to think straight. She's not trying to be annoying or make me mad, but I just don't feel like even being around her today, so I'm happy about this trip. She's standing almost right outside of the door, which kind of startles me, but I don't mention it. I walk right past her, grab my suitcase, and head out of the room to put my shoes on so we can leave.

"Are you okay? You're not acting like your normal self this morning" Emily says to me. I don't want to talk about it and I especially don't want to talk to *her* about it right now. I decide that it's best to just ignore her because if I don't, we're both going to be late to work because she will want to talk about it and fix it before we start the day. It's like she turns into a therapist the moment we argue. It's slightly obnoxious because it always turns into me being *"some type of way"* and her being right.

I finally got out of there and into my car. I reverse out of my parking space and make it onto the road. I flip through my CD case as I'm driving and I don't find anything I truly want to hear this morning, so I toss the case on the passenger seat and drive in silence.

I don't like cars with fancy GPS systems and screens on the dash. Even though I work in IT, I hate technology. Emily says that I'm paranoid, but I just know how technology works and it's way too scary for my liking. There's people out there that hack into systems everyday and track people, it's crazy. Emily watches shows like that and I don't know how she sleeps at night afterwards. Even when she's not watching it on the TV, I can hear true crime podcasts playing on her phone while she's showering or cleaning the apartment.

My phone buzzes, *"Do you want me to get your morning coffee ready for pickup?"* reads the text on my screen. I quickly answer back with a *"yes, please and thank you."*

There is a tiny coffee shop on the first floor of my job and the barista that is always there is Emily's best friend, Cecelia. Cecelia always has my coffee ready to go when I get inside, that way I can just grab it and go straight to work without waiting in the long line. People will be late to work just because they want the coffee she makes, but I don't blame them.

Maybe it isn't about the coffee. It's probably because Cecelia is a total smokeshow.

Chapter Three

Emily

I walk into the school and clock in. I don't say much to anyone as I'm feeling a bit confused about earlier and don't want to bring that to work. I put on my fake smile for those I pass in the hallway until I get to my classroom.

After I get all of the material ready for the day, I sit down at the piano and begin to play a small part of a song I heard on the radio.

I can't remember the name of it, but I liked it. That's a fun fact about me, I can remember notes and recite them flawlessly. The first date I had with Nathan, I told him I could do that and I spent the next two hours in my parents living room taking his song requests. It was so much fun. All of our dates were so much fun. They still are, but here recently he's been distant.

As I'm playing piano, Dan Bennett walks in. Dan is the gym teacher here at the school and I'm not going to lie, he is hot. Obviously I only think my husband is the best, but Dan has a great body and he's so sweet to me. He brings me a granola bar or a donut everyday from the teacher's lounge.

"Good morning, Miss Bates," he says. I always correct him because it's supposed to be Mrs. and not Miss, but today I don't. "How are you doing Dan?" I ask. "I'm okay, I'm just checking on my favorite teacher before class starts," he winks at me. I know it doesn't look good because I'm married, but what's wrong with some harmless flirting, right?

After chit-chatting for a little while, Mr. Bennett has to go since class is starting in about five minutes. Today is an early release day, so I feel somewhat better. My first period class is always the most relaxed class I have. They're still tired from the morning and they don't really have an interest in anything other than getting the class over with.

The bell sounds off and then I can hear nothing but footsteps and voices coming down the hallway. I step outside my classroom and I greet each and every one of my students. I think it's nice to greet them individually, that way they feel special first thing in the morning. My mother never made me feel special or beautiful and I think that's why I have such compassion for these kids. I would love to have my own kids someday, but with how Nathan thinks, I doubt that will ever happen unless I trick him into it, but that's totally wrong.

We've had the conversation about having kids, but Nathan is so scared that the baby will get kidnapped or die in its sleep. I get it, I really do because I'm sure every parent has those fears. I just don't understand how he couldn't get over that for me. He knows I want my own family someday.

"Good morning class," I say in the same high pitched voice I use on my husband every morning. "Good morning Mrs. Bates," they all say in unison. They all sound super tired as usual. I pull out my agenda for the day and then I put it back down. I don't want to do vocal warmups and I don't really want to teach them about music. I can't figure out why I feel this way, it isn't because of Nathan still, is it?

"So," I say, "I think we're just going to start a movie and watch it throughout the week." My class perks up at the thought of that, so I guess it works out for everyone involved. I have a small TV in my classroom, just like the rest of the teachers here, which I think is pretty cool. I turn on the movie "Sing" for them and I settle into my desk chair.

I sent out a text to my husband that asks *"Are we okay?"* He looks at my message, but doesn't respond until a few minutes later, *"Why wouldn't we be?"* What does he mean *"why wouldn't we be?"* He clearly ignored me this morning and was acting like he was mad. I'm so frustrated that I didn't even text him back, but instead I clicked on my best friend's name in my phone and sent her a text. *"Ugh!!!! Why are men so irritating?! All morning Nate has been an ass to me."*

Cecelia is my best friend and the one I tell absolutely everything to. We've been friends since before I knew Nathan. Her and I have known each other since kindergarten and Nathan didn't come along until middle school. He was always a nerdy guy, but it's progressively accelerated since then.

    My phone finally buzzes and it's Cecelia. *"Idk girl, he was super nice to me when he came in to get his coffee this morning."*

Chapter Four

Nathan

"*Are we okay?*" reads the text on my phone from Emily. Why can't she just leave this alone? I just need time to exist without being questioned, can't I just have a bad day and it be okay? "*Why wouldn't we be?*" I responded, but Emily never got back with me. I did in fact, get a text from Cecelia a few moments after I sent that text to Emily.

"Em is losing her mind, maybe you two should talk."

I do not want to talk to Emily about what's going on with me at all. I don't respond to Cecelia because I don't want anything on a paper trail that includes my marital problems.

As I head to my next meeting, I look at my watch and realize that I only have a certain amount of time until I have to be out of here for my business trip. I walk as fast as I can to this last meeting which will last approximately three hours, which is a little less than what Emily has left in her day. The school has an early release once a month and today is that day. I think it's pretty cool that her job has those kinds of days, I wish mine did. My day is just filled with meetings and a bunch of computer work. It gets tedious and a bit boring, but it's fine, it's what I love to do.

This meeting is boring, I want to leave already, but I can't because I'm speaking next.

We build and update the programs used in hospitals. Even though we warn the hospitals that we are updating and shutting the systems down for a while, some of them still get upset at us and complain. We get a lot of calls the morning after we update, which is okay, but annoying.

I do my part of the meeting and sit back down to listen to everyone else. After we all have our turn speaking, we usually go through the updated system and test it to make sure everything is perfect, which it is, per usual.

The meeting ends, but before I head out the door, my boss calls my name. I turn around and look at my watch once more, I have to go, but I can't ignore my boss. "What can I do for you, Mr. Stine?" I ask. "Well, your trip is cancelled" he says, "I know you were looking forward to that extra pay and time away from the ol' lady, but maybe next time bud." He pats me on the shoulder as he walks past me. He doesn't realize that it hurts me because I've been wanting to travel with the team for two years now. I had my chance today and it got cancelled. How did he know I wanted time away from Emily?

I chase after him, "Wait! Why is the trip cancelled?" Mr. Stine turns to me, "The trip itself isn't cancelled, you're just not going anymore." He starts walking away again, but this time I don't chase after him, I just stand there with my jaw almost on the floor. It feels like I just got punched in the heart. I want to text Emily about it, but I don't.

I don't even want to finish my workday, so I grab all of my stuff and I head back down to the lobby. I don't care if I get fired and I don't care if they call me, I'm not answering. I end up running into Cecelia on my way out of the door. "Hey!" she says, almost with that same high pitched voice Emily uses on me in the morning, "Are you okay?" I want to tell her that I'm fine and I can't wait to see Emily when I get home, but as soon as I open my mouth, everything that's bothering me spills out of it. I tell her all about my unhappiness with Emily and the fact that my boss crushed my dreams of going on this business trip.

"I'm so sorry, Nate" she says, grabbing my arm, "Let me walk you out to your car, I'm all done here today." I don't decline her offer and I let her hang onto my arm the entire way to the cars. Interesting enough, we are parked right next to each other. "I will..uhm..see you tomorrow" I say with a nervousness in my voice. The way that she was holding onto my arm made me feel different. The pain I had in my heart from my boss melted away with each step we took. "Of course you will, and your coffee will be nice and hot for you Mr. Bates."

Chapter Five

Emily

Finally, school is over and I get to go home. I'll be alone at home since Nathan is going on his trip, but my show is on later and I can relax with a candle and a book until then. My show is on an hour after I usually go to bed, but I'm making it a point to stay up late for it. Before I left school, I took a sick day for tomorrow and will have a substitute filling in for me. I never take sick days, but I just don't feel good mentally and don't want to pass that onto my students.

I pull into my parking space at the apartment building and sit there for a minute. I can see our window from my parking space. Did I leave that light on? I have watched way too much true crime, but I probably left it on.

As I go inside, I am extra cautious, even though nobody is in here. There's nothing to steal in here. Nathan hates technology, so we only have a TV and our phones. If it were up to him, we wouldn't have either of those things. We would be living like cavemen. Okay, that's dramatic, but still.

I open the fridge and see what I can make for dinner later, but there's only leftovers from the other night. They should still be good, right? I usually do the smell test, but there have been a few times that the food smelled fine and we still got sick.

I look in the cupboards next and there's nothing. I really need to go grocery shopping.

I finally give up and decide to order food for delivery. Nathan would have an aneurism if he knew I did this every so often. Before I can click the *order* button, a notification pops up on my phone: *Software Update Required.* Again, I click the *Update Later Tonight* option and toss my phone on the couch. The last few updates I've had lasted for twenty or so minutes, or at least it feels like it. I don't get why they just preload the phone with every single thing. Nathan would flinch at that statement, but he's not here so I can say whatever I want.

My food finally arrives and I sit down to eat. I look at my phone, it's 2 o'clock in the afternoon. I wonder if Nathan made it to his destination. I pull my phone out to check and see if he texted me. Nothing. I don't bother sending him a text, but I do want to text Cecelia and ask her about what she meant earlier.

"Hey girl, I know this is weird, but you said Nate was nice to you earlier. I know he should be nice, but it made me feel bad." I sent the text, anxiously waiting for a response. She finally answers, *"I didn't mean it in a bad way, but you two really should talk."* What does she mean by that? Cecelia has been very standoffish with me lately and I don't know why, so I ask her. She quickly responds with *"Em, I love you and I love being your friend, but the things you do aren't really within my beliefs and I don't think we should be friends anymore."* She then goes on to tell me that how I talk to her about the gym teacher at my school is inappropriate and that I shouldn't act like that if I'm married. This is coming from the girl who dated four different guys in college and got pregnant. She didn't know who the dad was and she had a plan to not tell any of them she was expecting. Unfortunately, but fortunately, she lost the baby within weeks. It was probably due to all the

drinking she did. I don't think she ever did forgive herself for that.

I decided that I want to take a short nap before I shower and get ready for the new episode of my show. I lay down on the couch and cover up with the light blue blanket I got for Christmas last year from Nathan and drift off to sleep.

I wake up just around 6pm and I feel like I slept for days. I set an alarm to wake me up at 4, but I guess it didn't go off. Must be the needed update, I guess. I don't know how any of that works and any time Nathan tries to explain it, I zone out.

I get up and fold the blanket, placing it back on its respective couch cushion. I go into the bathroom and undress to get ready for my shower. After turning on the water to let it warm up, I look at myself in the mirror. Again, I can see the weight that I've gained. I wouldn't be surprised if in a year, when I'm a glob of fat,

Nathan leaves me for someone who looks like a Barbie doll. I don't see myself working out and I don't really have the desire to fix my body. I feel self-conscious about it, but I'm fine just the way I am, or at least, that's what my mother would say before I disappointed my entire family by getting married to Nathan. Now she would probably look at me and throw up.

My shower felt amazing. I took a longer one than usual because my podcast was an extra long special episode. I love those, but they only do them every so often.

I grab the current book that I'm reading and go back to the couch. I check my phone again for a text from Nathan, but still nothing. No notification other than the pestering reminder that my phone needs to update.

Chapter Six

Nathan

I don't go home after I get off of work. I should have, but I didn't. I made a huge mistake and I'm not sure I want to go home and face my wife after what I did.

I went out and got drunk, but not only did I get drunk, I got drunk with Cecelia. I texted her after her car pulled out of the parking lot and asked her to meet me at the bar.

I struggled with alcoholism since I was a teenager. I would show up to school with a buzz and nobody would know it, I was a pro at hiding it from the teachers. Both of my parents were alcoholics, so I blame them. I know, I had the choice to keep dry, but I didn't and I blame everyone else for my problems.

Emily stuck with me through all of the drinking problems and relapses. I'm thankful for her, but every time I fell back into it, she looked more and more disappointed in me.

I was clean for a year before today. I was so proud of myself, but I threw it all out of the window just because I'm having a bad day.

"I appreciate you coming to meet me, Cece," I say. She nods her head, "I'll always be here for you and since Emily and I are no longer friends, it'll be so much better."

I absolutely should not think about cheating on my wife with her best friend, well, *ex* best friend.

Cecelia is the one who told me about Emily and Dan, the gym teacher. It angered me so bad, but I could never find the right time to talk with Emily about it. I didn't want to tattle on Cecelia, but I also didn't want to spend my life getting emotionally cheated on.

I've met Dan and he seemed like a good guy until he started bringing my wife donuts and granola bars. That's probably why she's gaining all that weight. That sounds incredibly rude, but it's true. I don't hate her for it because it doesn't matter, she never lets me see her body anymore. It's been about six months since we've had sex and she didn't really care for it then.

Cecelia and I exchange a few more words before we part ways. I get into my car and she gets into hers. Neither one of us should be driving, but if I die on my way home, I guess I really don't care. I would care if Cecelia got hurt, though.

I sit in my car for a while before I turn it on. I want to go home, but I also want to text Cecelia again and just have her meet me at a hotel. That's my drunk brain thinking and I know that, but it doesn't stop me from doing it.

"Hey, Cece. I know this might mess everything up, but do you want to get a room with me at the hotel on Ray Street?" I type out the message, but I don't send it. I just stare at it for a while. *Send.*

My heart is pounding inside of my chest. I can't believe I sent that message.

My phone dings, it's Cecelia. *"Nate, you need to talk to your wife. You know I would, but I can't be with a married man."*

I think of different ways I can ask Emily for a divorce, but none of them suit me. I think of just leaving her, but I can't do that either. She will worry and show up to my job, which will cause a ton of chaos that I don't need, especially if I want to try and travel with my team again.

I can definitely tell that I'm drunk because the only other thought I have in mind is just getting rid of Emily completely. True crime style. If she's gone for good, I can try to start over with my life.

I smack myself in the face. I should not be thinking about cheating on my wife and I really should not be thinking about killing my wife.

I back out of my parking spot and start driving. I don't know where I'm going yet, but just like before when I used to drink, I'll figure it out.

Chapter Seven

Emily

It's now 8pm and my show is starting. I have popcorn with M&M's mixed in and my tumbler cup full of water. I turn on the TV and the channel is already set to my station.

Nathan won't let me get a smart TV, so we're stuck with the TV that has commercials and no fast forward option unless you pause it for a while.

I love watching these true crime shows and movies. I also really love the podcasts that I have on my phone. I'm not sure what it is about them, they're just so interesting. I wish I could be inside one of the killer's brains for a day, just to see what goes on. Obviously, I wouldn't murder someone, but I would definitely let the thoughts flow.

Halfway through the show, another commercial comes on and I check my phone. Still no messages from Nathan about his business trip. No messages from Cecelia either. I kind of expected her to apologize for what she said to me, but she didn't. We've had fights in the past, as friends do, but this time was different. I think our friendship reached its expiration date.

Software Update Required. Oh my God, fine. I click *Update Now* and enter my phone password for the approval. My phone shuts off and begins the update. My screen is telling me that there is 21 minutes left on my update.

There's a nauseous feeling in the pit of my stomach. What if Nathan calls me with an emergency? What if I start choking on my popcorn and can't call anyone for help? We don't have neighbors next door yet. They're moving in at the beginning of next month. I won't make it down the stairs without passing out if I choke. What if the building collapses? Okay, now I'm being dramatic. If the building collapses, I'm dead anyways.

20 minutes left. Great, only one minute has passed.

My show is back on, which distracts me from the update. After about five minutes, I look back at my screen, 18 minutes left. 18 minutes? This is why I hate updates, it always lies about how long is left.

Usually I'm not worried when my phone updates because Nathan is here and we're going to sleep as it goes through the motions of getting rid of the latest bugs and changing how the keyboard looks. I know, I sound stupid, but I don't really know how these updates work.

16 minutes, 15 minutes, then back up to 16 minutes. What could they possibly be doing? I always imagine little robots in my phone during the update squishing big bugs and rearranging my stuff. I let out a giggle to myself.

I'm having a hard time getting into this episode of my show and I'm pretty sure it's because I stressed myself out.

Just then, all of my lights go out. And then my door flies open not even a minute later.

There is a masked man standing before me in my doorway and before I could let out a scream, he ran at me and covered my mouth with a microfiber cloth that smelled of car oil.

Chapter Eight

Emily

Holy shit. There is a masked man covering my mouth. I can barely get any air in or out of my nose as that's halfway covered up too. I'm hyperventilating. I strain my eyes looking at my phone, *14 minutes left.* Oh, my God. I'm going to die right here on my couch and nobody will know until Nathan gets home tomorrow night.

I took tomorrow off of work, so they won't know and Nathan isn't talking to me, so he won't be worried tonight.

"You're going to do everything I say and you're not going to make a sound. Got it?" the man says. I can't speak due to my adrenaline, but I nod my head yes. "Good, let's go to your room" he says.

He lets me go and I stand up. I very quickly thought about running for the door, but I didn't. I do as he says and I make my way into my room. I do believe that I peed my pants, but of all the true crime I've watched, it doesn't matter because he's probably going to kill me anyways.

Nothing happened for a few seconds, we just sat on the bed together. This is strange. Wouldn't he have started having his way with me already or killed me?

He's got a black mask on his face, I wonder how he can see. He's wearing a heavy coat and snow pants. It's hot outside, so I'm sure he's sweating pretty badly.

"Uhm," I say quietly, "If we could just forget about this and you leave. I won't call-"

"Shut up!" he screams at me.

I damn near jumped out of my skin. I'm not used to getting screamed at like that. I choose not to say anything else, even though I now know for a fact that I peed myself. I want to tell him that I need to clean up, but I don't want to be screamed at again.

I have never had someone break into any house I've lived in. I did grow up in a gated community, but even after living with Nathan outside of the gates, nobody has ever once bothered us. Nobody has ever even stolen from us.

I try once again to speak, but I end up getting yelled at some more. He then grabs a sock from my dirty clothes basket and shoves it in my mouth after tying my wrists to the bedpost.

Finally, this man turns his head to me and says "I don't want to hurt you, but I have to." He *has* to. What does that mean? Did someone hire him to take me out? Is this his first murder?

∼

I think that my phone is done updating and I know that if I run fast, I can grab it. I just won't have time to dial anyone. I need to figure out what to do so I don't get hurt.

What does he mean he *has* to hurt me? Hurt me as in beat me up or hurt me as in kill me. There are many different types of hurt, I just want to know what kind he means.

I really wouldn't tell the police or anyone if he just left me alone without hurting me. I want to tell him that, but he won't listen.

I managed to slip my hands out of the ties and for some reason, my body overpowered my brain and leaped off the bed. I spit out the sock that he gagged me with and I ran out of the room so fast. I didn't even stop for my phone, I just went straight for the door. I grabbed the handle, but I wasn't fast enough. He grabbed me by the hair and threw me down on the ground.

I look on the couch and my phone screen is black. Is it done updating?

I finally get free of his grasp and tap my screen. There is a bar that is about half full with the words *Updating* underneath of it. It's still updating and I can't call for help.

The man grabs me again and drags me across the floor by my wrists until we get back into the room.

How long has it been? It feels like hours, but I know it's only been a few minutes.

Chapter Nine

Nathan's Past

I grew up in a trailer park with my parents and sisters. I've always wanted a brother, but I never got one. I'm not complaining about my sisters, I love them, but they never want to do anything fun with me.

I usually go outside and find animals to catch. I like to kidnap the animals and take them in the house when my parents aren't home. I liked to put them in a cardboard box and see how long they struggled before realizing that they can't escape.

I wouldn't kill them on purpose, but some of them caused their own heart attacks. I released them as soon as they calmed down. I just liked to time different animals and keep a journal of it.

When my dad would get home from work, he would drink. He would always offer me some, but I would decline.

One day, I finally agreed and we got along better for those fifteen minutes of drinking a beer than we have in my entire life. It was fantastic until my mother walked in the door and saw an empty beer bottle in my hand and my pupils dilated out of my head.

My mother scolded both of us for at least twenty minutes before walking away. She drank too, so I'm not too sure why she got mad to begin with. I'm sure she would've eventually offered me a drink.

She still cooked us dinner and served it to us on the couch, but before I could take a bite, I threw up all of the beer plus some of my lunch. I feel horrible, but better at the same time.

"Looks like we have ourselves a lightweight" says my dad, "Go get cleaned up kid, I'll have your mom clean this mess up out here."

My dad usually treated my mom badly, but for some reason, she submitted to him. She never argued with him if he demanded something out of her and she never fought back unless she knew for a fact she was right.

My parents didn't beat me or my sisters, but they weren't very empathetic either. If we got hurt, it was always *"Get up and walk it off."*

I promised myself that I would never have children because I know that this type of behavior runs in my blood. I know that I'm going to be a drunk and I know that if I have kids, I'll act just like my father acts. I'll be lucky if I can get married to someone who's as patient as my mother is.

∼

After a few years of my dad progressively getting worse to my mom, she ended up fighting back one day and losing her life.

My dad killed her with his bare hands right in front of me and my sisters. He strangled her until the color and life drained from her face. He strangled her until her heart stopped and she quit breathing. It was terrifying, but satisfying at the same time. He never got caught because my mom didn't have anyone to care if she went missing or not.

After that day, I quit kidnapping random animals from the trailer park and I made a vow to myself that I would never do what my father did to my mother.

I don't want to kill anyone, especially the one I marry, but how do I stop myself? It's in my blood.

Chapter Ten

Emily's Past

    I grew up in a three story house with a finished basement. I had everything I wanted plus some more. My family included me, of course, my parents, and my brother. We also had a housemaid, a gardener, and a personal chef.

    We went to a private school along with the other kids in my gated community. My parents never thought to send my siblings and I to public school. My mom said it was filled with underachieved teachers and dirty people from trailer parks. But, once my school burned down, my parents had no choice but to send me to public school until they found another private school.

My best friend, Cecelia, was my neighbor. Her mother also sent her to the same public school as me so we could both have someone we knew around.

My mother never took me out of public school. My happiness went up and I think she noticed. I know my father wasn't happy, but he always said *"Happy wife, happy life."*

Cecelia ended up leaving public school and going back to private school. I did make a friend named Nathan, though. Nathan was a weird kid with his big glasses and backpack wrapped around both of his shoulders. I had to teach him how to be somewhat cool if he was going to hang around me without me becoming a laughing stock.

Nathan was never allowed at my house after the first time. My mother said his clothes looked like they came from a thrift store. They probably did, but who was I to judge? He was kind of cute.

∼

After a few years pass, Nathan and I start dating. We're going out every weekend together and we're *always* kissing each other.

My parents aren't happy with me, but they only want to see me happy, so they let it slide. Nathan's dad is over the moon happy, but

I'm not sure why. Nathan won't be marrying into money because I know how my parents are. The minute we get married, they're done talking to me forever.

My brother is now a drug addict and has been kicked out of our house. My parents aren't even trying to help him, so I won't be surprised if he ends up dead in a ditch somewhere soon.

Nathan ends up proposing to me after years of dating. I think he was trying to milk the homemade meals and a clean bed to sleep in. My parents let us sleep in the same bed, but with the door wide open. We're definitely not doing anything that she thinks we're doing, so I'm fine with it.

Nathan is very affectionate, but not into sex. I only asked about it once and he got upset with me. Not too upset, but upset enough that he didn't talk to me for a few hours.

Chapter Eleven
Cecelia

I've been calling Nathan's phone, but it goes straight to voicemail every single time. That means his phone is either turned off or dead.

After we left the bar, we were both a bit drunk. I'm worried about him because of what he said right before we parted ways.

Nathan broke down to me today and said that Emily wasn't making him happy anymore and he doesn't know why that is. He wants to be with her forever, but has caught feelings for me. That puts me in a mess because I also have feelings for him and I think he's known that for quite some time now. I just can't be with a married man. As soon as I told him that, I could see the gears turning in his head.

I know about Nathan's past and I know what he is capable of. I feel like I was an awful friend to Emily because of the amount of texts and conversations exchanged between Nathan and I. But, then again, Emily was always flirting with the gym teacher.

I want to go to the apartment, but I don't know if he actually went home or if he went to the hotel he invited me to. I definitely would've gone if he was divorced, but even though Emily and I aren't friends, I can't do that to her. I'm a loyal person to everyone, even if it makes me sad.

I sent a text to Nathan, *"I'm going to the hotel. Are you there?"*

No answer. The text message didn't even deliver.

I try to send other messages, but it's the same thing.

I end up driving to the hotel, but I don't see his car. I drive around the entire parking lot and still don't see it. I drive to a few bars around the area and his car isn't at any of those either. The only other option that I have is his apartment.

I think about it for a while and decide that I will just drive by, but not go up and see if he's there. If his car is there, I will go home and await his call or text. If his car is not there, I will have no choice but to call Emily and see if everything is okay. I'm worried about her anyways. Nathan's words shook me to the core.

I take the ten minute drive to Nathan's apartment. He lives out of town in a not so countryside, but countryside apartment building. It's a beautiful building, but it still looks somewhat run down. I heard that's what the owner of the building wanted.

I pull into the apartment parking lot and there's his car. It's not parked in his usual spot though, it's parked in the corner spot where his neighbor would park if he had a neighbor.

I park in Nathan's normal spot and send him a text, *"Nate, I'm outside your apartment and I know you're here."* I wait and wait for an answer, but I don't get one. Again, it doesn't even say it got delivered.

I don't think it's best that I go in, so I start to drive home. All I can think about is what Nathan said to me: *"I think Emily is better off dead."*

Chapter Twelve

Emily

    The man throws me onto the bed, my wrists feel broken. He tied me up again and shoves that nasty sock back into my mouth. When he grabbed them, they both felt like they popped out of socket. I can still feel my fingers and rotate my wrists with some pain, so I think I'm okay for now.

I've never had strong joints or bones. I used to pop my elbows out of socket and sprain my wrists and ankles all of the time as a kid. Through all of the tests I've done, they can't find anything wrong with me.

I just want to know what he wants from me. I'm nobody special and neither is my husband. We have nothing to steal and we have nothing to give. We aren't rich by any means, so any money I give him wouldn't even be enough to buy a Big Mac meal.

Nathan and I make good money, but not enough to have a luxurious lifestyle. We split the bills in half and by the time everything is paid for and groceries are bought, we only have enough left to put gas in the cars. Sometimes Nathan will work overtime at his IT job and give me a portion of it for food delivery when he knows he will be late. Even though he doesn't like it when I give out our address to random food delivery apps, he always makes sure that I'm fed and happy with what I ate.

The man sitting on my bed looks at me and says "I don't want to kill you, I have to kill you." There's a familiarity in his voice that makes me feel sick and calm at the same time. I can't quite put my finger on what the familiarity is.

Once again, I get out of the ties and my body takes over. I jump off of the bed and back out to the living room. Again, I spit out the sock. Just as I make it out, I see my phone lit up with a text message. Before I can reach it, the screen blackens and the man grabs me from behind.

"You bitch!" He yells at me as he's dragging me back to the room again.

My heart is pounding out of my chest. I am the most scared I've ever been in my life. What does this man want from me? What did I do to him?

"I'm sorry, please just let me call my husband" I say, knowing he won't let me. It created a sense of comfort knowing that I told him I was married. I don't know why, but my heart told me to throw that information out there.

He ties my hands to the bedpost once more. This time, I know I'm not getting out of it. He tied my wrists to this bed so tight that it feels like it's cutting into my skin. I want Nathan to come and rescue me so badly. I want my husband to bust in the door and take down this man who is causing me so much pain. He won't. Nathan isn't the fighting type.

I can hear my phone start ringing in the living room. The man jumps, it's almost as if it startled him.

He gets off of the bed and out of the room. He's grabbing my phone. I hear him shuffling around in the living room and in the kitchen before he walks back into the room.

This man is literally holding my lifeline in his hands right now and I have no access to it.

"Who..called me?" I cautiously ask. He never put the sock back in my mouth, thank God. He turns toward me, "Cece." My heart sinks into my stomach and a huge wave of nausea comes over me. I lose my dinner all over myself and the bed. If I wasn't tied up, I could've at least made it to the trash can next to my bedside.

That's another thing Nathan didn't like, my trashcan next to the bed. I love to snack at night and that always grossed him out. He didn't like me eating in bed, but I never got crumbs in it. I'm extremely careful.

It breaks my heart that Cecelia called my phone and I couldn't answer. She probably called to say that she wants to apologize and be my friend again. Well, that's what I want. I truly think our friendship is over, but a girl can hope.

I never wanted to lose Cecelia as a friend. I told her everything and she told me everything. We are, *were,* best friends.

There is one mistake this man made and that was not putting that sock back in my mouth. I let out the loudest, most blood curdling scream I could.

That is the biggest mistake I could have made.

Chapter Thirteen
Cecelia

Not even a few seconds after I pull out of Nathan's apartment building, I see flashing lights behind me, I'm getting pulled over.

As I'm sitting on the side of the road waiting for the cop to come talk to me, I remember that I've been drinking and this cop is definitely going to know it.

The police officer finally gets out of his car and starts walking up to mine. He's an old cop with a big belly, I could outrun him if I wanted to, but I won't. A DUI only lasts a person a night in jail if they're not usually in trouble with the law.

"License and registration, please."

I have never heard a police officer use the word 'please' in my entire life. They're usually so rude and straight to the point, but I guess they have to be for their line of work.

I hand over my license and registration and to my surprise, he says "thanks, I'll be right back." This is the nicest cop I've ever met.

I sit for at least five minutes and during that time, I'm worried sick because it shouldn't take this long, should it? I didn't do anything wrong. Maybe someone stole my identity and committed a crime and now there's a warrant out for my arrest.

I have to talk my nerves down because that scenario is not plausible at all.

Finally, he's coming back with my stuff.

He hands me my license and registration back. "Have you been drinking today, ma'am?" he asks. I knew that was coming. Even I could smell myself, plus I spilled a shot on my leggings, so that didn't make me smell any better.

"Uhm" I say, but before I could finish my sentence and come clean about the fact that I was drinking, his radio beeps and the voice that comes over his radio said something that shook me to my core.

"There is a disturbance at the Courtside apartment complex in apartment 225."

225? That's Nathan and Emily's apartment number. This has got to be a mistake.

The voice on the radio continues, "All units please respond."

All I can do is look at the officer with tears in my eyes.

"You're free to go," the cop says before rushing back to his car.

My heart is in my stomach, I don't know what to do. When a dispatcher says *"All units please respond,"* that never means anything good.

All I can do now is drive away and go home. *What have I done?*

Chapter Fourteen
The Masked Man

Before I knocked Emily's door down, I found the main breaker box in the hallway. I assume it's for the maintenance guy if he needs to cut power for any reason. They really should put a lock on it because it's easily accessed, but it's not my problem that people are ignorant.

Of course, I flip the switch for the apartment Emily is in before kicking her door in. I'm thankful the door ricocheted and made a complete close, I thought I broke it.

I didn't give her enough time to panic or scream before I covered her mouth with a cloth I found in my trunk.

Emily is a fighter, I'll give her that. But, unfortunately, there was no way for her to successfully escape me.

I tied her up and she did get out a couple of times, but I was always faster and stronger. It was pure luck that her phone was updating and that she wasn't on the line with someone.

I made a huge mistake by not gagging her after her last escape attempt. I thought she had given up. I didn't think she had any fight left in her, but I was totally wrong.

Emily lets out a scream that deafens me for a few seconds. It was so loud and high pitched that I'm sure the downstairs people heard it. I'm pretty sure the next state over could hear it too, it was *that* loud.

I panicked after that because it was only a matter of time before someone came to make sure she's okay. A scream like that isn't one you hear when someone is just playing around.

I had no other choice but to grab her by her throat and strangle her until she stopped breathing.

It was just like how my father killed my mother.

It was oddly satisfying to watch the life drain out of her eyes. Her skin color turned a few different shades of blue and purple before I let her go.

I had every reason to kill her. Not because she screamed, but because she was a whore with the gym teacher. I don't know if they slept together, but the way they acted around each other made me sick.

I wanted Emily to feel how I felt and that's why I was going after Cecelia. I wanted her heart to hurt the same way mine did when I saw my wife giving special treatment to a man who doesn't deserve it.

Emily will never know that her own husband, the masked man, killed her.

Chapter Fifteen

Cecelia

There is a knock at my door that makes me jump. I hesitate to open it because I'm scared that it's the cop coming back to take me away to jail for my DUI.

After a few seconds of thinking, I get up and answer the door. It's Nathan and he is sweating and out of breath.

"Please let me in, Cece" he says, panting. It looks like he's about to blow a blood vessel or pass out. I've never seen someone look like this.

Of course I let him in and before I can say anything, he tells me everything. He tells me how he disguised himself and broke into his own apartment. He tells me how he tied Emily up and basically tortured her until he finally killed her.

"Why didn't she try to call for help?" I ask. That's the only thing I can manage to ask. Emily is dead and instead of worrying more about that, I'm worried about why she didn't call for help. I am such a bad friend.

"Her phone was updating" Nathan answers.

The luck that Nathan had is unbelievable. He does work in IT, so I doubt that he didn't know something was going to go on with her phone. Maybe he had no idea at all, but he was smart enough to figure it out for his timing.

"Nate, what are you going to do?" I ask him, hoping he tells me that this is some sort of sick joke Emily is pulling to get me back for ending our friendship.

He shrugs, "I don't know."

He doesn't know. Of course he doesn't know because who would know their next step after killing their own wife? Unless you're a professional serial killer, which Nathan is definitely not.

"Cece, I don't want to ask you this.." Nathan says, taking a deep breath, "Will you help me hide?"

I am appalled. He's asking *me* to help him hide. I have never hidden someone in my life, where do I even start. Why am I thinking about helping him? He killed Emily.

Before I can ask any questions, Nathan grabs my hand, "Please, Cece, I need you."

This breaks my heart, he really needs me. I want to help him, but I don't want to get caught in the crossfire and end up in prison with him. There's no way he's getting away with this, nobody ever gets away with murder. Do they?

"I'll help you, but we need to move fast" I say, hesitantly. *This is not going to end well.*

Chapter Sixteen
Officer Connor

I respond as quickly as I can to the apartment building, but I really should've given that girl a ticket for drinking and driving. I should've been able to make an arrest, but when all units are called to respond, I have to drop everything I'm doing no matter what. It's a small town, so I couldn't really wait for backup from another city to come take over.

I walk into apartment 225 and head back to where the other officers are. In this town, this kind of stuff doesn't happen. Murder doesn't happen.

It's quiet here and there's never usually any disturbances unless the Wilson's from the creepy house outside of town get too mad at each other. They're an old couple with no kids. They either love each other or hate each other, it depends on the day.

There is a girl laying before me, eyes closed and her face is drained of color. There is no doubt in my mind that she's deceased.

"So, what happened?" I ask, assuming that there's not much detail.

Officer Mainley looks at me and says "Looks like a break in. Based on how the door looks and the marks on her neck, it appears to be a break in gone wrong."

I make it clear that this doesn't look like a random break in and murder type of situation. This looks to be a decision based on emotions.

Officer Mainly and the other officers who joined agree.

Detectives and crime scene units show up and at this point there is nothing more I can do other than help keep people away from the scene. I wish I could do more, but now it's up to the detectives.

Chapter Seventeen

Nathan

Before Cecelia and I officially go on the run, I make her drive past my apartment. I know that there is a huge risk of me getting caught and her getting pulled over, but I just need to see it one last time for my own sake.

As we get closer, all we can see is a bunch of flashing lights and a bunch of cops and crime scene people.

"Turn off" I say. I don't want to go past it anymore. I know that they're in there looking at what I've done. I'm ashamed of myself. I should've never done that, but I had to. She was no good, she was a cheater and she didn't love me. If she did love me, she never looked at me with the amount of lust in her eyes as she did with the gym teacher.

Cecelia turns off and looks at me with a worried look, "Nathan, where are we going to go?"

At this point, I'm not sure because I'm afraid to call anyone. I don't want anything on a paper trail from my phone because I know the first person the cops are going after is me.

"My parents have a cabin a few hours from here," Cecelia says.

Of course they do, Cecelia grew up rich, just like Emily did. I don't understand people that have multiple properties. I could never keep up.

"Can we go there?" I ask. Cecelia takes a breath and I can see on her face that she's thinking. "Let me call my mom," she says. I try to tell her that it's not a good idea, but she insists that it's fine.

While Cecelia is on the phone with her mother jabbing away, all I can think about is the look on Emily's face as her life was coming to an end. All she wanted was me at that moment. Little did she know, she had me. She didn't know that the man in the mask was her husband, her protector. She will never know.

"My mom said it was okay for us to go to the cabin, but we can only stay for a month because she's renting it out to a family for a week next month" Cecelia says, tossing her phone back into the cupholder.

I'm relieved, but a bit scared that Cecelia just left a trail of her and my whereabouts with someone I know will hear about my wife being murdered. If her mother puts two and two together, not only am I screwed, but Cecelia is screwed too.

"Cece, I need to ditch my phone" I say. Before she can object, I throw it out of the window and into a huge ditch filled with water.

"Are you out of your damn mind, Nate?" Cecelia yells at me, almost stopping the car. "Keep driving Cece. When we're in the clear, we can stop and get me a burner" I say. Not that I'll need another phone. Nobody called me but my job and my wife, and then Cecelia when we got close.

∼

We finally make it to the cabin and it's spooky out here. It's dark by the time we arrive and we're in the middle of nowhere.

I get this weird urge in the pit of my stomach and this tingle in my hands. I think my adrenaline is pumping back up, but I have to ignore it.

"Here we are," Cecelia says, sounding somewhat excited, yet relieved. "Should we go in?" I ask. That's such a stupid question, of course we're going in. We're not going to sleep outside.

As we enter the cabin, I feel calm and alone. I feel like nobody can find me out here. It makes my heart relax.

Cecelia comes up and stands next to me, "There are some men's clothes in the closet upstairs and the shower is up there too." I'm thankful for this information because I feel horrible and dirty.

I head upstairs and undress. Before I get into the shower, I look at myself in the mirror. I don't even recognize myself, I look like a complete stranger. I shake it off and give myself a light tap on the cheek before getting into the shower.

While I'm showering, I feel the tingle in my hands again. *What is this?* It feels like they want to grab onto something and squeeze until I can't squeeze anymore.

That's when I remember that Cecelia is downstairs.

Chapter Eighteen

Cecelia

Nathan is taking forever in that shower. I would also like to shower because I need to wash the guilt off of me. Is that even possible?

"Nate!" I yell, "Are you almost done up there?" No answer. I go up the stairs and into the bedroom that is connected to one of the bathrooms, "Nate?"

He startles me by walking up behind me. "Sorry, I was looking for some clothes," he says. "Why didn't you answer me?" I ask. He just gives me a dirty look before saying "I'm sorry, I didn't hear you."

I feel bad for scolding him, but I'm on edge. I'm sure he is too, but I'm more on edge because I'm hiding a literal murderer from the police. I should be terrified of him, but I'm not.

"I think we need to try to relax. Is there any TV out here?" Nathan asks me. I point downstairs, "My parents just installed a smart TV in the family room."

I can see the annoyance in his eyes, but he doesn't say anything. Emily mentioned that they weren't allowed to have a smart TV or any technology for that matter because Nathan was scared of hackers or something.

As we head downstairs to watch TV, my phone buzzes in my hand, *Software Update Required.*

I look at it for a moment deciding if I should let it update later or if I should just get it over with now. I hover my finger over the screen and click *Update Now*. I type in my passcode and then my phone shuts down.

The End.

www.ingramcontent.com/pod-product-compliance
Lightning Source LLC
LaVergne TN
LVHW041541070526
838199LV00046B/1776